Cosmo
THE DODO BIRD™

Cosmo THE DODO BIRD™

Cosmo is a dodo bird, a unique species that lived on Earth 300 years ago. Cosmo lived with his family and beloved friends on the island of Mauritius, a paradise isolated from the world known to man.

When the first humans arrived on the island, the dodos' environment changed vastly, and it wasn't long before almost all of the dodos completely disappeared.

Now, Cosmo is the last of his kind on Earth.

3R-V is a small robot-spaceship from the future, built to save extinct species. During his very first mission, he accidentally landed on Mauritius and met Cosmo, the last of the dodos. They decided that they would travel the universe looking for dodos. They found many adventures along the way, but did they discover any dodos? Read and find out!

Originally published as *Les Aventures de Cosmo le dodo de l'espace: La planète filante*
by Origo Publications, POB 4 Chambly, Quebec J3L 4B1, 2008

Concept created by Pat Rac.
Editing and Illustrations: Pat Rac
Writing Team: Joannie Beaudet, Neijib Bentaieb, François Perras, Pat Rac

This English edition published in Canada by Tundra Books, 2011
75 Sherbourne Street, Toronto, Ontario M5A 2P9

Published in the United States by Tundra Books of Northern New York,
P.O. Box 1030, Plattsburgh, New York 12901

Library of Congress Control Number: 2010928802

Library and Archives Canada Cataloguing in Publication
Pat Rac, 1963-
[Planète filante. English]
The traveling planet / Patrice Racine.

(The adventures of Cosmo)
Translation of: La planète filante.

ISBN 978-1-77049-242-4
I. Title. II. Title: Planète filante. English. III. Series: Pat Rac, 1963- .
Adventures of Cosmo.

PS8631.A8294P5313 2011 jC843'.6 C2010-903175-X

We acknowledge the financial support of the Government of Canada through the Book Publishing Industry Development Program (BPIDP) and that of the Government of Ontario through the Ontario Media Development Corporation's Ontario Book Initiative. We further acknowledge the support of the Canada Council for the Arts and the Ontario Arts Council for our publishing program.

ONTARIO ARTS COUNCIL
CONSEIL DES ARTS DE L'ONTARIO

For more information on international rights, please visit www.cosmothedodobird.com

Printed in Mexico

1 2 3 4 5 6 16 15 14 13 12 11

MIX
Paper from responsible sources
FSC® C101537
FSC www.fsc.org

For all the children of the world

THE ADVENTURES OF

Cosmo THE DODO BIRD™

THE TRAVELLING PLANET

TUNDRA BOOKS

Table of Contents

CHAPTER ONE

A Radar Problem

We have been traveling through space for ages looking for dodos. You see, I'm the last of my kind, and I would give anything to find another dodo like me. 3R-V and I had visited one planet after another, and we'd had many adventures and met lots of odd characters. But we still hadn't found any dodos, and then we couldn't even find any other planets!

I was bored. It was hard not to be, when all I could see was space and stars. To pass the time, I counted the stars: 775 . . . 776 . . . 777 . . . Soon that game stopped being fun. I wished we'd come across a planet to explore.

I could tell that 3R-V was as bored as I was. The little robot-ship was gliding through space with his eyes half-closed. Every now and then I heard a loud *mpuff-mpuff-mpuff*. He was snoring. When he started to veer off course, I tapped on the capsule.

"3R-V, wake up!" I said.

"Eh! What's happening? Have you seen a planet?"

"No. You were sleeping, my friend."

"Oops!" 3R-V rubbed his eyes.

That bit of excitement didn't last long, and soon I was bored again. I tried blowing on the glass to make a mist. I drew a planet on it with my wing.

I tapped the radar screen to see if it could detect any signs of life. Suddenly, a point flashed on the screen. 3R-V noticed it right away.

"Cosmo, there's a planet on the radar!" he exclaimed, wide awake.

"Hooray!"

"Whoa! Something's wrong! The radar's not working properly," said 3R-V.

"How can you tell?"

"It indicates that the planet is already behind us."

"But we haven't passed a single one!" I said.

I crossed my wings and worried. If the radar was broken, could we have missed other planets?

An alarm rang in the cockpit, and a red light flashed.

"What does that mean, 3R-V?" I stared at the radar screen.

"It means danger, Cosmo!"

The light continued to blink rapidly. On-screen, the planet looked like it was charging straight at us.

"3R-V! If your radar is correct, the planet will pass under us in five . . . four . . . three . . . two . . . one–"

To the second, a big orange planet sped out in front of us. The robot-ship squinted at the planet. "I see trees and water, Cosmo. It looks tropical, just like Mauritius!"

"There might be dodos! Quick, 3R-V, try to catch up to it before it gets too far away."

We followed the speeding planet, and we could hardly see anything. 3R-V dodged between small bits of glimmering space debris.

Once the dust cleared, the planet was way ahead of us.

3R-V set out after it, but the planet was faster than he was. Soon 3R-V was going at his top speed. The stars flashed by. Would we ever catch up to the planet?

CHAPTER TWO

Déjà Vu

At last we entered the planet's atmosphere.

"Phew!" said 3R-V. "This planet can really move! A little faster, and we would never have caught up to it!" He brought us to a safe landing.

While I leapt to the ground, an exhausted 3R-V checked his robotic legs and hands to make sure no parts had fallen off.

"I'm sure I've never been here before, but I feel like I recognize this place, don't you?"

3R-V looked around. "You're right, Cosmo. The twisted trees, the orange sky, the deep jungle, and the ragged mountains all seem familiar!"

The thick jungle reminded me so much of home that I couldn't wait to explore it. I brushed against the giant leaves to hear the familiar swishing sound. I touched the twisted trunks of the trees. I inhaled the smell of the jungle. "I have a feeling of déjà vu!"

All of a sudden, we heard raised voices. 3R-V and I tiptoed toward the sound. We stopped at the edge of a clearing.

Standing next to an enormous machine was a strange creature with two-heads. The heads were quarreling. I took a few steps closer so I could hear.

“Right, you took my yellow screwdriver!”said the left head.

“I did not, Left!” cried the right head.

“That’s not true,” grumbled the left head. “You’re always taking my tools to make your works of art. Admit it! You took my screwdriver!”

“I did not! You probably lost it.”

"I always put away my tools properly, Right!" The left head was huffy.

"Maybe you melted it down for one of your experiments."

"Melt my favorite yellow screwdriver? Never," the left head said.

That was when I remembered why the creature was familiar. 3R-V had told me the story of the two-heads creature. The robot-ship's mouth was open. He recognized it too.

"Are you the two-heads?" I called. "*The* two-heads from the *Tale of Two-Heads*?"

The creature jumped.

"A tale?" asked the left head. "What tale?"

"You remember, Left! I made it up myself. Just think. *The Tale of Two-Heads* has traveled right around the universe!" marveled the right head.

"What's it about?" asked the left head.

"It's the story of you and the last flower on your planet," I reminded Left.

"Oh! That story! All the flowers disappeared, except for one."

The two-heads smiled, and I thought about the story.

The two-heads formed one creature. The right head was artistic and had a lively imagination. The left head was scientific and logical.
They used the same special kind of flower for their art and for their science. The flowers were so plentiful that the creature didn't notice it had used them all up.
All except one, that is.
"It's the last flower so it belongs to me!"
"Don't touch it. It's mine!"

The creature was so busy arguing with itself about which head should get the last flower that it didn't realize the flower was starting to droop.
Finally, one morning, the right head noticed something was wrong.
"Look, Left, it's shedding its petals."
"We have to save it!"
The creature took care of the small flower, and it came back to life.
Once again, there were blossoms everywhere.

"See what happens when we work together?" said Right. The two-heads decided to call the flower Hope.

I was still thinking about the story when I found myself speaking aloud.

"I can imagine how beautiful the flowers were."

The right head stretched toward me.

"You don't have to imagine it. Come. There is a field of flowers close by." The creature grabbed one of my wings. "But you should know that the flowers talk. Gossiping is their favorite pastime!" Right said.

We had only taken a few steps when the left head stopped us. "Hold on! Who did you say you were?"

CHAPTER THREE

A Planet Out of Orbit

"I'm Cosmo, the dodo bird. This is my friend, 3R-V."

The left head studied the robot-ship.

"What an incredible invention!" it exclaimed.

"I am specifically designed to save extinct species," explained 3R-V proudly. "I'm helping Cosmo find other dodos."

"I'm afraid there are no dodos on our planet. Sorry," said Left, who could see that I was disappointed.

"That's true. I've never seen a dodo!" added Right.

I was sad, but I wasn't surprised. I was sure I'd been on this planet before and found no dodos. I was even convinced that I'd searched the same jungle.

"We've already been here," I told the creature.

3R-V shook his head. "That's impossible, Cosmo! We were in another galaxy far away."

3R-V was right, but I still felt sure that I'd been to this planet before. I scratched my beak. Was I crazy?

As if reading my mind, Left spoke: "You're not crazy! Our planet didn't always travel in space."

"How did it end up so far from your galaxy?"

"A galactic tornado–" began Right.

"–in our solar system," added Left.

"The tornado grew before our very eyes," Right continued. "It grew until it was bigger than our planet – bigger than our galaxy!"

I tried to imagine a tornado that big.

"We were drawn into its center." The left head took up the story.

"How long did you spin inside the tornado?" I asked.

"Days and days. And then, *BANG!* The tornado stopped, but we kept spinning. Before we knew it, we were far from our galaxy. We've been racing through space ever since."

"What bad luck!" exclaimed 3R-V.

"Not at all!" said the two-heads. "We love our traveling home. We keep finding new galaxies!"

"New stars!" said Right.

"New planets!" said Left.

"Do you often see new planets?" asked Cosmo hopefully.

"From time to time," said Left.

"I love to paint them!" the right head said happily.

"And I love to explore them to search for new discoveries!" added the scientific left head.

"They are on a mission like ours!" I said to 3R-V.

"Here's an idea!" cried the heads. "Why don't we *all* travel together? The more the merrier!"

"That's not a bad idea," said 3R-V. "Cosmo, you get bored during our journeys in space. If you lived on this planet, at least you'd be surrounded by nature."

I thought about what my life would be like on the traveling planet. I'd have a jungle to run through, streams to swim in, and a leafy nest to sleep in. It was easy to make up my mind.

"Let's do it!"

“How do you go about searching for new planets?” I was curious.

The two-heads pointed to a contraption a little way off.

“Ta-da! This is my invention!” said the left head.

“You mean my work of art,” said the right head.

The two-heads started bickering again.

I interrupted it. “But, what is it?”

Together the heads replied, “It’s a telescope!”

CHAPTER FOUR

Surprise!

3R-V and I were impressed.

"What do you think of my work of art?" demanded the right head.

"Don't start that again, Right. It's an in-ven-tion!" said the left head.

"A work of art!"

"An invention!"

While the two-heads argued, I looked through the lens. Everything was black.

"Your telescope doesn't work," I muttered.

"Work of . . . *What*?" cried Left. "It just needs to be adjusted."

While Left fiddled with the mechanism, Right took up a paintbrush.

The two-heads stopped bickering and worked peacefully. So as not to disturb it, I climbed on a rock. Everything was perfect: the green jungle, the rugged mountains, the warm sun, and the orange sky. I smiled at 3R-V.

"I love this traveling planet! We can all live happily here."

The right head heard me.

"Oh! You haven't met our grouchy neighbor, yet."

"We're not the only ones here?" I was excited.

"The yellow screwdriver!" both heads exclaimed at the same time.

I was confused. "The yellow screwdriver lives here?"

"No, no, no," said Left. "We just remembered! He borrowed my yellow screwdriver this morning–"

"To adjust his helmet!" finished Right.

"We are so scatterbrained!" the heads said together and laughed.

CHAPTER FIVE

The Search for the Jewel

The two-heads signaled for us to come, and we followed. It squabbled while it walked.

"You see, I didn't take your silly screwdriver!"

"And I didn't lose it!"

"Do you ever stop getting on your own nerves?" demanded 3R-V, exasperated.

The two-heads giggled. "Getting on my own nerves!" it said. "That's a good one!"

We all laughed.

We soon arrived at the foot of a rocky hill. Menacing warning signs were scattered everywhere. I didn't dare move a feather.

The two-heads didn't seem to be put off by the signs that said: DANGER and OFF WITH YOU and DO NOT DISTURB.

"I don't think he wants visitors," I whispered, pointing at the signs.

"Worried about the welcome signs? Ignore them," said the left head.

I did worry, so I followed on tiptoe. No point in startling somebody who sounded so crabby!

The two-heads stopped at a door in the rock face. It knocked lightly.

"*Grrr!* Who goes there?" growled a voice from inside the hill.

"It's your favorite neighbor!" said the right head.

"What do you want?"

"Could I please have back my yellow screwdriver?" asked the left head.

The door opened a crack. The yellow screwdriver appeared.

The two-heads stuck a foot in the doorway.

"Wait! I want to introduce my new friends to you."

"Friends? I don't see any friends!" growled the voice.

The two-heads opened the door wider and pushed 3R-V and me inside.

Standing there was Diggs!

"Cosmo, is it you?" cried Diggs.

"It's me. What are you doing here?"

"Do you know each other?" asked the right head.

"Yes! We've been to his planet."

"Perfect!" said the left head. "In that case, I will leave you! I have work to do on the telescope."

"I'm with him! There are still plenty of parts for me to paint."

With that, 3R-V, Diggs, and I were alone.

"How did you end up on the traveling planet?" I asked.

"I could ask the same of you two," Diggs snapped.

Although we had become friends, I didn't know he was such a grouch. "We discovered this planet by accident. It nearly bumped into us," I explained.

"Now tell us how you got here," asked 3R-V.

"I sold my jewel," said Diggs.

"What? You sold your planet!?"

I thought about Diggs's planet and our adventure there.

On our travels through space, we'd seen a planet that looked promising. When we tried to land on it, 3R-V had a hard time finding anywhere to plant his feet. The ground was full of holes!
We met Diggs, who dug those holes in his search for a hidden jewel. The more holes he made, the more fragile his planet became.
"Soon, I will be rich, rich, RICH!"
"I'll be the richest person in the universe!"
I tried to warn Diggs that his search was destroying his planet, but he wouldn't listen. I told him what 3R-V and I had seen before we'd landed there.

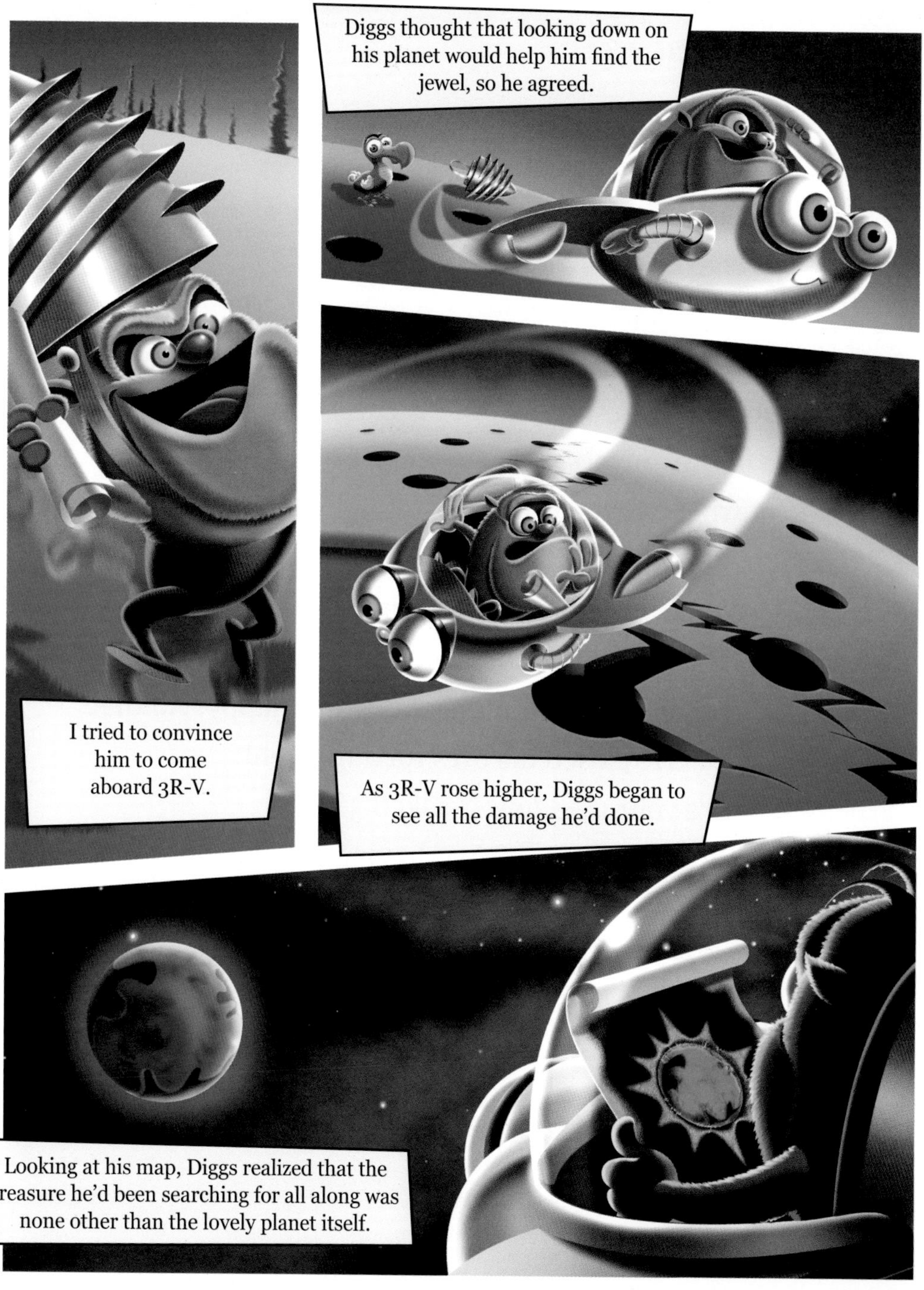
I tried to convince him to come aboard 3R-V.
Diggs thought that looking down on his planet would help him find the jewel, so he agreed.
As 3R-V rose higher, Diggs began to see all the damage he'd done.
Looking at his map, Diggs realized that the treasure he'd been searching for all along was none other than the lovely planet itself.

How could he have sold the planet he loved!

"Diggs, why?"

"It's simple, Cosmo! I wanted to be rich, rich, RICH!" Diggs's eyes sparkled. "I sold my planet for a mountain of gold pieces." Diggs puffed out his chest. "I was the richest person in the universe!"

"But what did you do after you sold your planet?" I asked.

"*Grrr!* You've put your finger on the problem." Diggs paused. "I had to leave and wander in space with my big sack of gold pieces. I was alone, but I was happy! All that lovely gold!" He closed his eyes for a moment.

"Where's your gold now?" asked 3R-V.

"I'll tell you." Diggs enjoyed having an audience.

"One night, as I was traveling through space," he began, "I saw a menacing galactic tornado gathering."

3R-V and I waited eagerly for him to go on.

"Before I knew it, I was caught in the storm." Diggs continued. "I was frightened. The storm cloud swirled; dust and debris scattered this way and that."

Diggs drew in his breath and slowly exhaled before continuing.

"The galactic tornado tossed me in every direction. The wind lashed me in the face. Rocks hit me on the head. All I could think to do was grip my bag of gold pieces with all my might."

"What happened next?" I couldn't wait to hear.

"Suddenly, a jagged rock hit my bag and tore through it!"

Diggs paused to catch his breath. “My gold pieces scattered everywhere in space. Then, everything became calm. Too calm! No more rocks or wind.”

“Was the storm over?” I asked.

"No! I had reached the eye of the storm, at the edge of a black hole! My heart thumped in my chest. The black hole was sucking me toward it. Worse, it was sucking up my gold pieces!"

"What did you do?" asked 3R-V.

"What could I do? I was helpless. All my gold pieces had disappeared!" Diggs shook his head. "I felt another rock hit me on the back. That made me mad. I turned and grabbed it. I was ready to throw it in the black hole when I realized that it wasn't a rock after all. It was a piece of gold!"

Diggs smiled and continued his story. "I hid the gold piece in the palm of my hand. Then I waited for the black hole to swallow me."

"How did you survive?" I couldn't wait to find out.

"The two-heads appeared."

3R-V narrowed his eyes. "What was the two-heads doing out in a storm?" he asked.

"I know!" I cried. "It must have been the same galactic tornado that propelled its planet out of its galaxy!"

"Exactly," said Diggs. "The traveling planet spun around the tornado. When the two-heads saw me in the middle of the storm, it flew to my rescue."

"Your story has a happy ending," I told Diggs. "You survived the storm!"

"But my treasure didn't," grumbled Diggs. "I managed to save just one gold piece. My precious piece of gold! Every time I look at it, I tell myself that one day, I will be rich, rich, RICH again! All I want is to be rich."

I shook my head. Diggs would never change.

"Where is the gold piece?" wondered 3R-V.

"If you think that I would reveal that secret, you are wrong," said Diggs angrily. "It's *my* treasure!"

All of a sudden, we heard loud voices.

CHAPTER SIX

One Eye on Space

"What is that racket?" Diggs went out to investigate.

"It sounds like the two-heads," said 3R-V. "What is it making this time?"

"It must be the telescope," I said. "Maybe it's fixed." We ran outside.

I climbed aboard the robot-ship as fast as I could. Diggs tapped a code on his helmet. I was puzzled.

“My experience in space has taught me one thing: It is important to have good tools at hand. Every day, I learn how to use my helmet as a different tool,” Diggs told us.

As he spoke, his helmet twirled in the air and became a rocket. We took off to find the two-heads.

“If the telescope is finally ready,” said Diggs, “we can use it to search for hidden treasure. Soon, I will be rich, rich, RICH!”

I was as excited as Diggs. The telescope might help us to find other planets – and other dodos! We spotted the two-heads and went to it. Diggs shoved it aside and looked through the telescope's lens.

"I see the stars in space!"

3R-V tapped Diggs's shoulder. "May I look, please?" he asked politely.

"*Grrr!*"

The two-heads gently pushed Diggs away from the telescope and offered 3R-V a turn. Diggs sulked.

"It's incredible!" exclaimed the robot-ship. "The stars are so beautiful. I feel like I'm back in space."

"My invention works perfectly!" the left head said proudly.

The right head cleared its throat.

"Oh, I know," said the left head. "It's an invention *and* a work of art!"

"Take a look, Cosmo!" 3R-V said.

I bent over the telescope. Diggs and 3R-V were right; the view was magnificent. It was as if I was inside 3R-V, drifting through space. I moved the telescope in every direction and tried to find familiar stars. Suddenly, I saw something that was larger than a star. I cried out, "Look! There's a planet!"

Left put its eye to the lens and adjusted the telescope. "You're right, Cosmo! We'll soon pass it." Left did some quick calculations.

"We're being propelled through space so quickly. Will we be able to visit the new planet?" asked 3R-V. "Our planet will travel right past it!"

"It is all a question of orbit, 3R-V!" explained Left.

We listened carefully.

"When our traveling planet crosses another planet's path, it enters into the other's orbit," Left said. "We'll circle the planet once, but then, we'll be propelled back into space."

The left head bent over the telescope again and zoomed in on the planet.

"Oooh!" it whispered.

"What, what, what?" we all asked.

"There are monsters everywhere!"

"Monsters!" we repeated.

I took Left's place and peered through the telescope. It was true. I could see monsters on the planet.

Among them was a small purple fellow.

"Hey, that's Fabrico!"

"What?" said 3R-V. "I can't believe it!"

"It's Fabrico's planet. And it looks like he's in danger."

"Quick," shouted 3R-V. "Climb aboard. We have to help him!"

CHAPTER SEVEN

A Hasty Departure

I hopped aboard 3R-V, while the two-heads kept watch on Fabrico's planet through the telescope.

"We're making our orbit around the planet now. As soon as we've completely circled Fabrico's planet, we'll shoot back out into space. You don't have much time to save him."

Left handed 3R-V a strange stopwatch. "Put this around your wrist."

"When all the bands are black," explained Right, "our traveling planet will exit the orbit of the new planet."

"Good luck," the two-heads called.

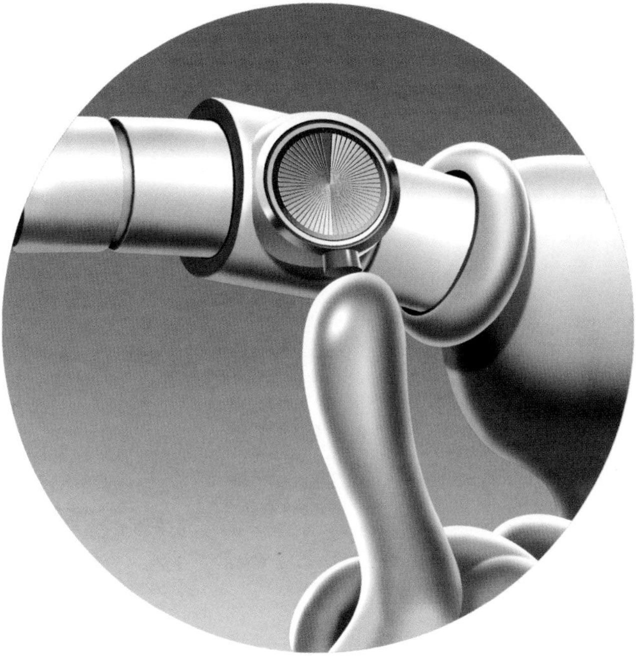

Before we took off, I called out to Diggs, "Are you coming with us?"

"Are you kidding? That place looks gross," he answered. "Those monsters slobber. Yuk!"

I shook my head. There was no changing Diggs.

As we flew through space, I remembered our visit to Fabrico's planet.

During our search for dodos, we'd landed on a lovely, grassy planet.
We met a workman named Fabrico, just as he was about to dump green slime into a river.
3R-V and I eyed the scary goo suspiciously.
What's this strange substance?
"I don't know. I am not paid to think!"
"See, the substance isn't dangerous!"
We told Fabrico that what he was doing was dangerous. To prove that it wasn't, he had put drops of the goo on a harmless little lizard's tongue.

Suddenly, the lizard turned into a terrible monster!
The effects of the slimy goo wore off, and the lizard went back to normal.
From that day on, Fabrico was changed. He promised to warn other workmen about the dangers of dumping substances into clean water.

CHAPTER EIGHT

Monsters Everywhere

As we landed, I was jolted out of my memories. Would we get to Fabrico in time to rescue him?

We entered the planet's atmosphere and saw monsters swarming everywhere.

3R-V flew toward the river where we'd seen Fabrico through the telescope. We tried to stay behind the clouds so that the monsters wouldn't spot us.

"Are you ready, 3R-V? Those monsters look pretty scary."

"Don't worry, Cosmo. I'm strong and nimble."

"Help!" We heard Fabrico cry out.

The brave robot-ship charged straight at the monsters. At top speed, we flew between the feet of a chubby creature covered with warts.

Another monster was waiting for us in midair – a winged creature with a dreadful pointed stinger!

"Watch out, it's chasing us!"

"Don't worry, Cosmo," 3R-V reassured me.

The robot-ship was headed straight for a rock face, the winged monster right on our heels.

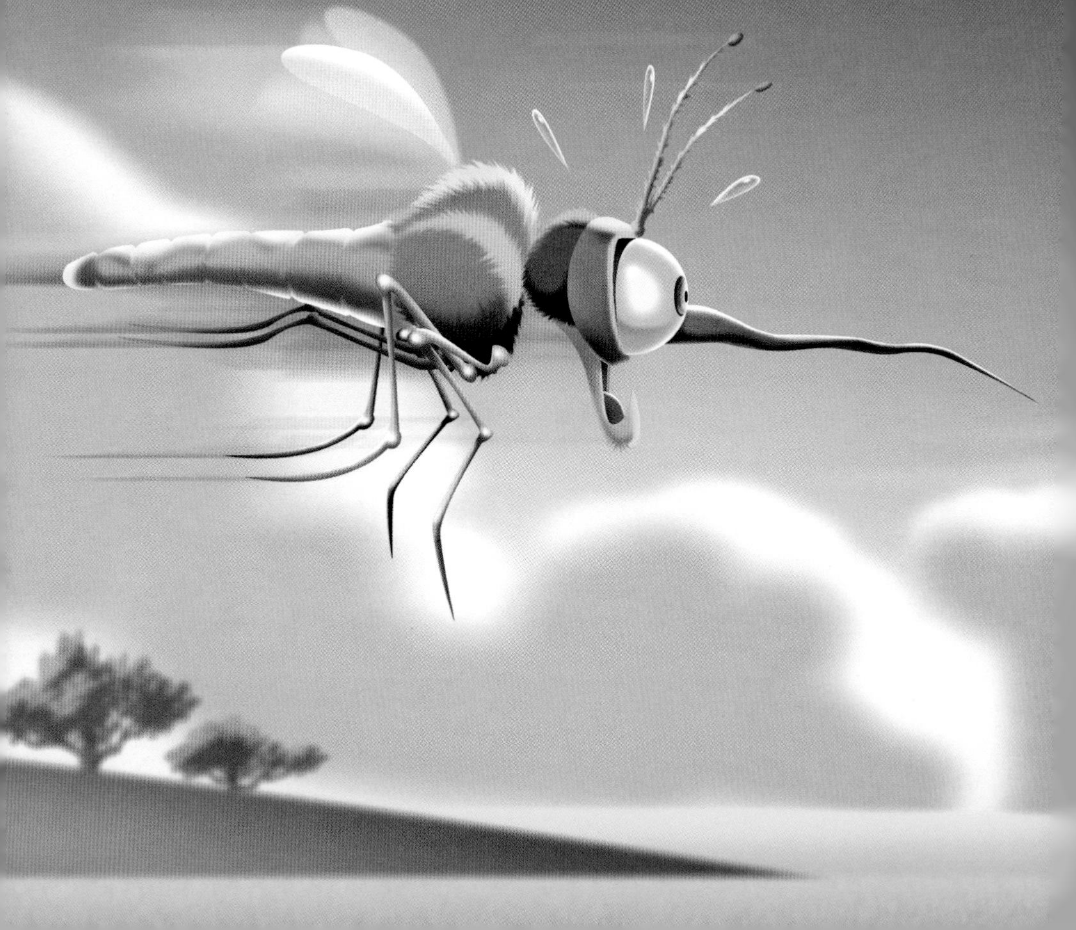

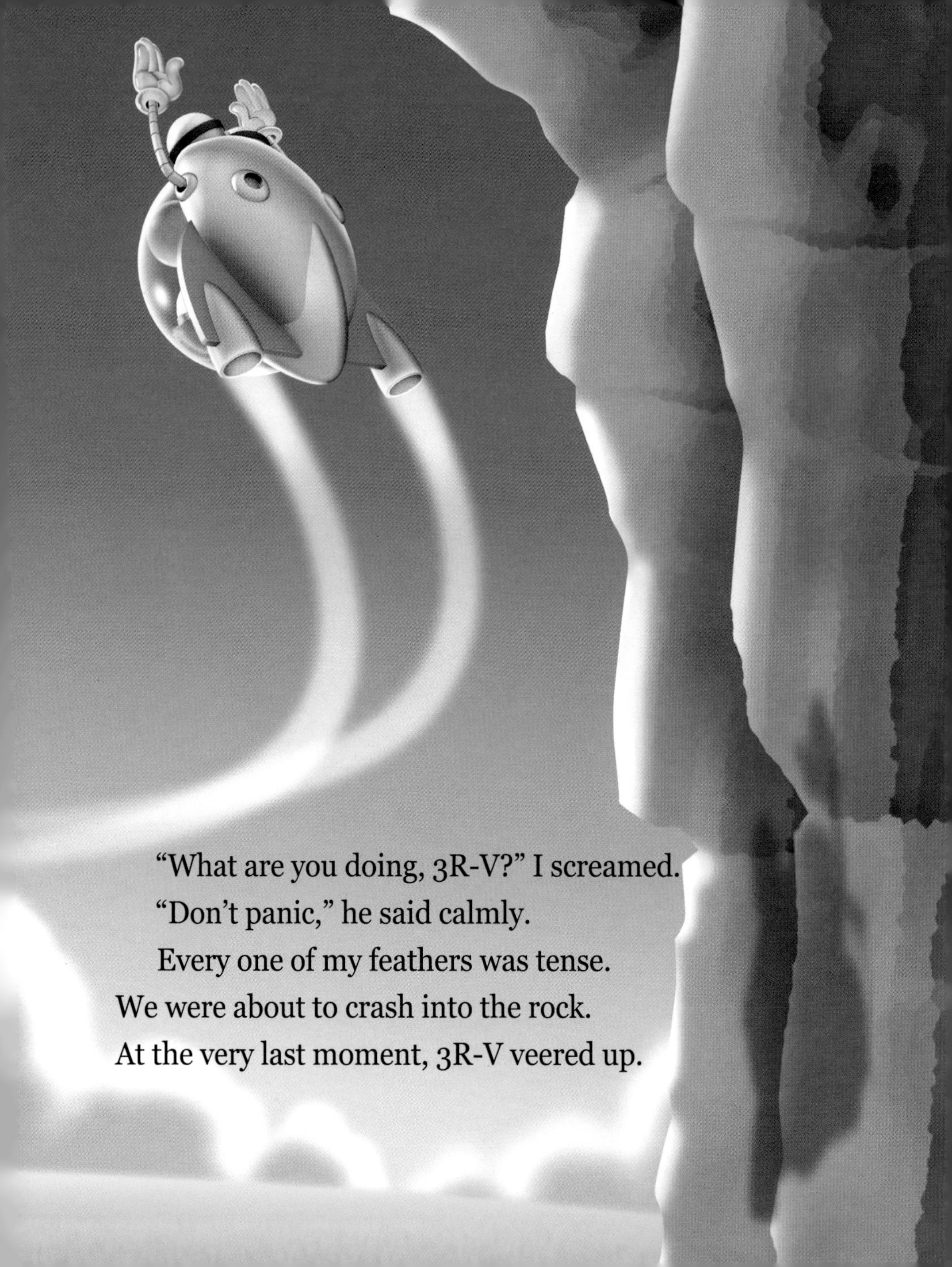

“What are you doing, 3R-V?” I screamed.

“Don’t panic,” he said calmly.

Every one of my feathers was tense. We were about to crash into the rock. At the very last moment, 3R-V veered up.

The monster was not as nimble as 3R-V. He splattered onto the wall.

"Bravo, 3R-V!"

"Help!" yelled Fabrico.

"Quick, 3R-V, every second counts!"

The robot-ship charged toward Fabrico. Suddenly, something slimy caught us in full flight.

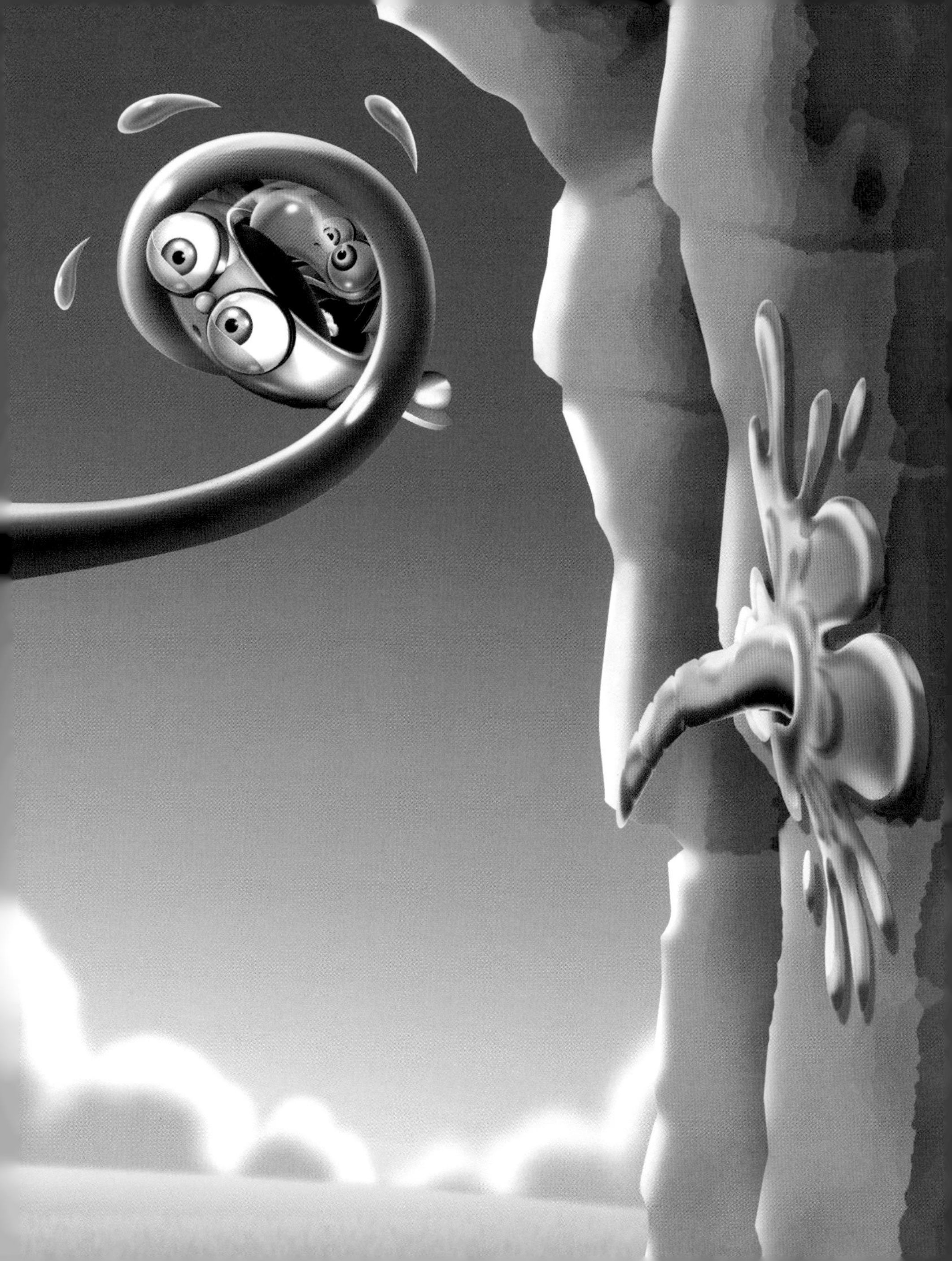

Its tongue wound itself around us and pulled us toward its razor-sharp teeth. We found ourselves inside the mouth of the creature!

"Oh, no! It's going to eat us!" shrieked 3R-V.

Its teeth chomped down, but they were no match for 3R-V's amazing, strong body.

With an angry snort, the monster spit us out.

BEEP, BEEP, BEEP! An alarm sounded inside the robot-ship.

"Uh-oh!" yelled 3R-V.

"What's happening? Did the monster harm you?" I shouted.

"No, the noise is coming from the stopwatch. We have to get back to the traveling planet! We only have seconds left!"

"But we can't abandon Fabrico!"

"Cosmo, we have to go back right now. If we don't, the planet will be too far away for us to catch up with it."

BEEP, BEEP, BEEP, BEEP, BEEP! The alarm rang urgently. Time was running out.

Suddenly, the monsters scattered.

"What's happening?" shouted 3R-V. "Fabrico!"

But Fabrico had disappeared! All that was left was his yellow helmet.

"It's too late." 3R-V sounded like he was ready to cry.

BEEP, BEEP, BEEP, BEEP, BEEP, BEEP!

"We can't stay here, Cosmo! It's too dangerous."

We left Fabrico's planet without him.

CHAPTER NINE

Jiggs or Diggs?

We had had a wild race against time, and time had won. We were miserable when we landed back on the traveling planet.

3R-V checked his stopwatch. The bands were almost all black. In a few seconds, the traveling planet would exit the orbit of Fabrico's monster-filled place.

I dragged myself out of the robot-ship, tears rolling down my cheeks.

"What happened, Cosmo?" the left head asked gently.

"It's our friend, Fabrico. He was eaten by a monster."

Suddenly, a purple fellow appeared.

“What?! I was eaten by a . . . a . . . monster?” our friend stammered. “But I feel fine!”

“Fabrico, you’re alive!

I threw my wings around him and gave him a big hug.

"Of course I'm alive! But I can't breathe," he grunted.

I loosened my grip.

"How did you escape?" asked 3R-V.

"The monsters had me surrounded. I didn't have a way out, and there was no escape. I was stuck, boxed in – "

"You were trapped," 3R-V cut him off.

"That's it!" cried Fabrico.

I shifted from foot to foot. Fabrico was a terrible storyteller.

"Suddenly, the ground trembled beneath my feet. *Brrr! Brrr! Brrr! Brrrrr! Brrrrr!*"

Fabrico rocked back and forth to show us, until I pleaded for him to go on with the story.

"Come on, Fabrico. What happened next?"

"Where did I leave off?"

"The ground trembled," prompted 3R-V.

"Oh, yes! And then, I said to myself, 'Oh, no! There's another monster beneath my feet!'"

Fabrico acted the whole thing out.

"But what happened?" I asked.

"It wasn't a monster after all," said Fabrico.

"What was it then?" said 3R-V impatiently.

"It was none other than . . . Jiggs!" shouted Fabrico, his arms in the air.

"No!" replied the left head.

"Not Jiggs – Diggs!" The right head corrected Fabrico.

"Oh yes! Diggs! He came up out of the ground right beside me. When he saw the monsters, he ducked back into his hole. I dived in after him. We crawled through his tunnel until we could come out safely. Then he brought me here."

I was amazed. Diggs rescued Fabrico?

"He is my hero!" exclaimed Fabrico. "Jiggs saved my life."

"Diggs," repeated the right head.

"That's what I said," said Fabrico. "If it weren't for DIGGS, the monster would have eaten me!"

"Cosmo and I were there too," 3R-V reminded him.

"Yes, yes. But you didn't do anything useful. Jiggs did everything."

"Diggs," said the two-heads wearily.

I was confused. How did Diggs get to Fabrico's planet?

CHAPTER TEN

A Little Giant Lizard

Fabrico couldn't stop singing Diggs's praises. "Diggs is so courageous!" he said, beaming with admiration.

3R-V shook his head. No doubt about it, he was miffed too. After all, 3R-V had been very brave when he faced the monsters to save Fabrico, and Fabrico had hardly thanked him.

"There were monsters all around me," Fabrico went on, "and yet Diggs was still able to rescue me!"

When he stopped to take a breath, I spoke up.

"Fabrico, what were monsters doing on your planet in the first place? I thought that you were going to warn the other workmen about the dangers of dumping strange substances into the river."

Fabrico's shoulders sagged. If the purple creature could have blushed, he certainly would have.

"When you left my planet, I ran to the factory with the little lizard and told everybody about what happened. I warned them that the slime was dangerous. The others stared at me as though *I* had two-heads." He looked at Left and Right. "No offense meant."

"None taken," the heads said together.

Fabrico continued. "One of the workmen said 'This lizard became a monster?'

'Yes! Yes! With pointy teeth!'

'And big claws?' asked another.

'And a menacing stare?'

The workmen looked at each other. Then they all started laughing. They pointed at me and made fun of me. That's when I had my brilliant idea. I dipped the lizard in the slimy goo."

"You did what?" I couldn't believe he would do something so silly.

"I dipped the lizard in the strange substance," Fabrico mumbled.

"Fabrico! You knew what would happen! How could you be so foolish?" I said.

"But nobody believed me! They laughed at me."

I shook my head. Fabrico continued his story:

"Well, I dipped the little lizard, and, sure enough, she became a monster. 'See.' I said. 'Now do you believe me?'"

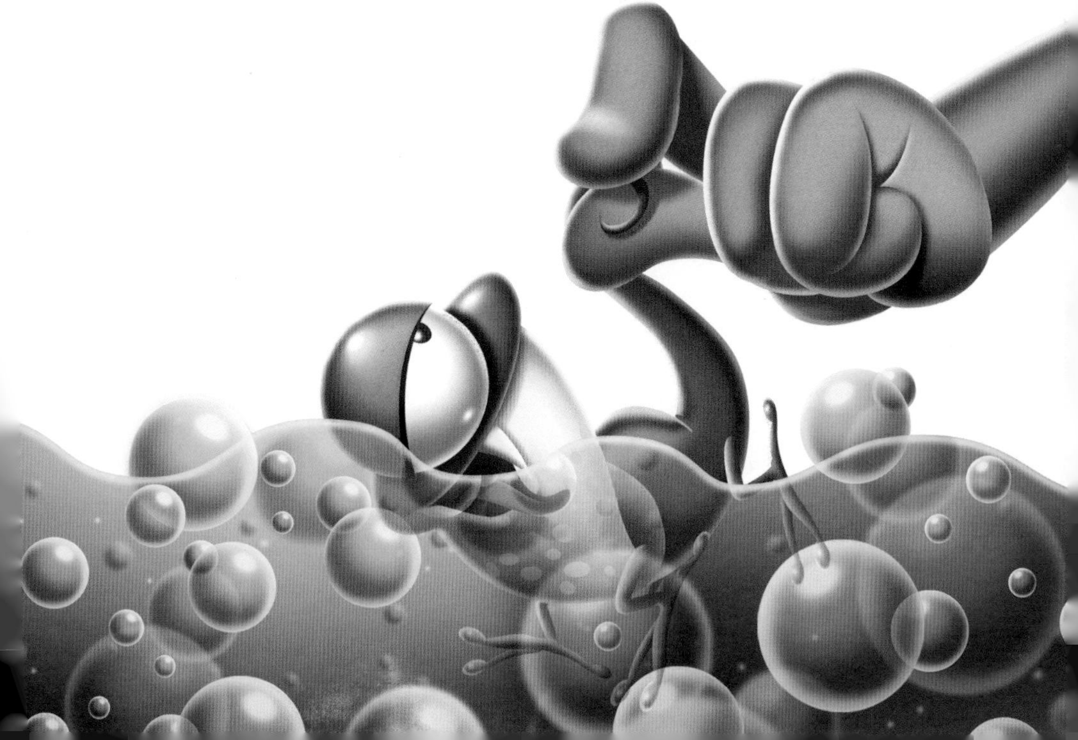

"The monster roared. *Grroooaar!* It was mayhem, I tell you. But at least they believed me.

And that's when everything went wrong. The monster leapt at the workmen, ready to eat them. Her tail hit the beaker filled with the strange substance, and the liquid spilled into the river."

"The whole planet was contaminated. All the animals and plants turned into monsters.

The factory had to shut its doors. All the workmen had to leave the planet because there was no work to do. Everybody blamed me. They called me names and said mean things. They said I ruined the planet. Fabrico stopped his story and wiped tears from his eyes.

"You know the rest of the story. I was the last person to leave. But before I could, the monsters attacked me – that's when Diggs rescued me. My hero!" he sighed.

CHAPTER ELEVEN

One Word Too Many

Fabrico looked around. He could tell that we were already far from his planet, too far ever to return. He sobbed as though his heart would break.

"Don't be sad, Fabrico." The right head tried to console him.

"From now on, you can live with us," said the left head.

Fabrico sniffled and snuffled and finally dried his eyes. "Thank you, thank you, thank you, thank you, thank you!" He hugged the heads. He hugged 3R-V. And then he gave me a huge hug.

"Now it's my turn to say that I can't breathe!" I squirmed until he let me go.

"Oops!" he apologized, grinning. "Hey, has anybody seen Diggs?"

The two-heads said, "He's probably at home right now."

"Where does he live?" said Fabrico.

"Over there," 3R-V pointed the way.

"Why do you want to see him?" I asked.

"Well, Cosmo, after he rescued me and dropped me off on the traveling planet, he disappeared. I didn't have the time to thank him."

I was confused. First Diggs refused to go to Fabrico's planet. Then he did go, and he saved the purple fellow. But then he disappeared without a word. I had many questions to ask. Instead, I said "Follow me. I'll take you to his house."

We left the two-heads fussing over its telescope. The short walk took a long time because Fabrico stopped every few steps to exclaim about the wonders of the traveling planet. "Look! That tree is twisted! Have you seen an orange sky before? What is that big leaf? Is this a fruit you can eat? *Yuk*! No! It's horrible."

When we were halfway to Diggs's hill, Fabrico strayed off the trail. He was soon back, bursting with news.

"There is a field of flowers over there. It's so beautiful! Come and look."

He led us through forest to a clearing. Pink flowers blanketed the ground. I recognized them from *The Tale of Two-Heads*. They were the hope flowers.

Fabrico bent over one.

"Hello, little flower!" he murmured. He turned to us. "Talking to flowers helps them grow," he explained. He touched the flower gently. "You are very pretty."

"Thank you," the hope flower hummed back softly.

We were astonished.

"The flowers! They . . . they talk!" said Fabrico.

"We talk. We whisper. We hum," said the sweet voice.

"Remember what the right head told us? The hope flowers can talk," 3R-V said.

"You are quite right, 3R-V!"

"They're not monsters, are they?" Talking flowers made Fabrico nervous.

"Look at them, Fabrico!" I reassured him. "The hope flowers are harmless."

The sweet voice piped up. "We are pretty and peaceful."

Gingerly, Fabrico sniffed a flower. “And you smell good!”

“Our scent is divine.”

“You see. There’s nothing to be afraid of,” I said.

Fabrico nodded. He danced through the fragrant, blooming field.

“I was worried for nothing! There are no monsters on the traveling planet.”

CHAPTER TWELVE

The Monster Tamer

No sooner had he spoken when we heard a terrible sound. Fabrico jumped into 3R-V's arms.

"Help! A monster!" he cried.

"What was that, Cosmo?" said 3R-V.

"The sound came from Diggs's house!"

Fabrico, now back on two feet, was too afraid to move, but 3R-V and I ran to the rocky hill that was Diggs's home.

"Don't go!" he called after us. "There's a monster in there! Save yourselves!"

"Diggs might be in danger, Fabrico!" I yelled.

"Diggs? My hero? In danger?"

"Why didn't you say so?"

Fabrico shot past us, and we followed as fast as we could. We were at Diggs's door in no time. I knocked loudly. "Diggs, are you there?"

No response. Fabrico pressed his nose against a window.

"Nobody is moving about inside."

3R-V inspected the ground around the house. "I can make out footprints – little ones *and* big ones."

"Where do they lead?"

"Take a look, Cosmo. They go up . . ."

Before 3R-V could finish, another roar rang out.

"The sound is coming from the top of the hill!" said 3R-V.

"Quick! Let's go!"

I heard another noise. *Clack! Clack! Clack!* I turned to Fabrico. His knees were knocking.

"You don't have to come with us," I said.

"I can't abandon Diggs." He gritted his teeth and took the lead. We climbed the hill in single file.

Fabrico froze every time he heard a noise. Each time, he had an excuse: "Sorry, it's only my stomach rumbling" or "that bird call surprised me" or "'a rock, I caught my foot on a rock. It could have been a monster."

"3R-V, why would there be a monster on the traveling planet?" I asked quietly, so that Diggs couldn't hear.

"I have no idea!" replied 3R-V.

The monster's growling grew louder as we climbed the hill. When we finally got to the top, sure enough, there was a monster in a cage. Fabrico scratched on 3R-V's hatch.

"Open up, 3R-V. Let me hide inside you."

"Calm down, Fabrico!" said the robot-ship. "There's nothing to be afraid of. See? The monster is locked up."

"I recognize this monstrous lizard! It was chasing me before I was saved! Who . . . who . . . captured it?" stammered Fabrico.

ROARRR

"Why, it's none other than me!"

"Diggs!" 3R-V and I shouted.

"My hero!" cried Fabrico.

Diggs was holding a small stool in one hand and a whip in the other.

"What are you doing here? Go away!" he rumbled.

"You captured this monster all by yourself?" asked Fabrico.

Diggs grunted that he had.

"You're a real hero! Not only did you save my life, but you captured a monster!"

Fabrico hugged Diggs and tried to kiss him. "Thank you! Thank you! Thank you!"

"*Grrr!* Let go of me!" complained Diggs, and he shoved Fabrico away. "Off with you! If you want to see the monster, you have to pay like everyone else!"

I frowned at Diggs. "See the monster? Pay? Who is everyone else? What are you talking about?"

"I'm talking about my circus, of course.
Diggs's Grand Circus!"

CHAPTER THIRTEEN

Diggs's Grand Circus

"You've opened a circus on the traveling planet?"

"Why do you think I captured this monster?"

I shrugged my shoulders.

"To get rich, of course!" he continued. "I tamed this creature so that people will come by the millions to admire it. I'll be rich, rich, RICH!"

"That's why you were on Fabrico's planet?" I was stunned. "Just to make money from this monster?"

"Exactly!"

"And to save me, don't forget," added Fabrico.

"I didn't really have a choice!" replied Diggs. "You followed me into my hole. Then, you jumped on me. To get you to let me go, I brought you here."

The monster rattled the bars of the cage.

"See," said Diggs. "With this monster, Diggs's Grand Circus will attract crowds!"

"Crowds? On this peaceful planet?" The idea troubled me.

"Isn't it a brilliant idea?" boasted Diggs. "This roving planet moves from one galaxy to another. A true traveling circus! Imagine our arrival to each new place!"

Diggs bowed to an invisible audience: "Hear ye! Hear ye! Diggs's Grand Circus has arrived in your galaxy. Come one, come all to admire the illustrious Diggs, Monster Tamer."

ROAR

The hideous creature roared and flashed its large, pointed teeth.

3R-V, Fabrico, and I jumped back. Suddenly, the monster went quiet. It shivered once, and huddled at the back of the cage. It belched loudly. Green bubbles floated out from its mouth.

Diggs's giant monster wriggled and slithered and wriggled some more. It was becoming a little lizard again!

"The substance has lost its effect!" I cried.

Stunned, Diggs peered at the little lizard.

"My . . . my . . . my monster!" Diggs could hardly speak.

"Are you all right, Diggs?" asked 3R-V.

"No! Of course I'm not. Without my monster, I will never become rich! Nobody will even cross the street to see this . . . this . . . tiny lizard!" Diggs stomped away.

The lizard slid between the bars of the cage and followed him. When Diggs looked back and saw the little creature behind him, he growled, "*Grrr!* Go away, you worthless lizard!"

Diggs took a few steps. The lizard took a few steps.

"Off with you!"

The lizard strolled up to Diggs and licked his foot.

"She's adopted you," I said.

Diggs shook his leg and cried, "*Yuk*! Lizard slime. Go away, I said!"

But the little creature stayed with him.

"Hmm," said Diggs, giving the lizard a wary pat. "I suppose you'll be a good guard animal. And, of course, I do have a treasure to protect."

The lizard stuck out her tongue, content.

The sun was setting as I settled into my nest on the edge of a rocky cliff. 3R-V was close by. I looked out over the planet. The telescope stood pointing up at the sky, right where the two-heads had left it. I thought of 3R-V and my newfound friends.

Each of us had lost our home, but had come together on this traveling planet.

We had been given a chance to start all over again. I looked at the orange horizon. "I think we'll be happy here."

"I think you're right!" 3R-V replied. "Rest up. There are more adventures to come."

THE ADVENTURES OF
Cosmo
THE DODO BIRD
CARING FOR THE ENVIRONMENT
THE QUEST OF THE LAST DODO BIRD
THE ADVENTURES OF
Cosmo
THE DODO BIRD
CARING FOR THE ENVIRONMENT
THE TRAVELING PLANET

THE QUEST OF THE LAST DODO BIRD

The last dodo bird on Earth, Cosmo is running for his life when something amazing happens. 3R-V, a robot-spaceship from the future, hurtles down from space and rescues him. 3R-V's mission is to travel back in time and save endangered species from extinction. 3R-V and Cosmo, set off to explore the universe in search of other dodos.

THE TRAVELING PLANET

Cosmo the dodo bird and his friend 3R-V find and land on a traveling planet that has been blown out of its galaxy by a huge galactic tornado. Before they know it, they, along with a strange group of castaways, are in for excitement. The new friends learn from each other and realize they have been given a second chance to protect their new environment.

THE ADVENTURES OF
Cosmo
THE DODO BIRD
THE CLIMATE MASTERS
THE ADVENTURES OF
Cosmo
THE DODO BIRD
THE CHAIN REACTION